Published by Two Lions, New York

www.apub.com

Amazon, the Amazon logo, and Two Lions are trademarks of Amazon.com, Inc., or its affiliates.

ISBN-13: 9781662508042 (hardcover)
ISBN-13: 9781662508059 (eBook)

The illustrations are rendered in digital media.

Book design by Abby Dening
Printed in China

First Edition

2 4 6 8 10 9 7 5 3 1

To the children of the world and all those who love them:

May you come to know that loneliness is just a call from deep inside.
And as you meet your very best friend in the mirror,
may that call transform into a shower of love that lasts forever.
–P. K.

To all the lonely kids, even the one I used to see in the mirror.
–K. H.

Ruby had a problem. But she didn't tell anyone about it.

None of the other kids at school seemed to have a problem like hers. They ran and played, and no one appeared to notice Ruby at all.

No one else in Ruby's family seemed to have a problem like hers.

Her older brother and sister were always off doing stuff with their friends.

Mom was always busy making phone calls at her desk.

Dad was always at his work, too, and when he came home, he just relaxed on the couch and watched TV.

Even her dog, Lola, didn't seem to have a problem like hers. Lola was always busy barking at birds and chasing squirrels in the yard.

And so Ruby sat there, day in and day out, alone with her problem.

And her problem was just that—Ruby felt all alone.

Ruby did not like her problem one bit!

One day at school, her teacher,
Mr. Garcia, talked all about problems.

"If you ever have a problem,"
he said, "it's best to examine it
from all angles and give it a name.
Then you can solve it."

But Ruby had no idea how to examine her problem from all angles.

It wasn't like she could pick it up and roll it around . . .

or hold it in her hands to show it to someone . . . or look at it with a magnifying glass.

This made Ruby's problem seem bigger than ever.

At the end of the day, Mr. Garcia came over to Ruby.

"Ruby, if you ever need help solving any of
your problems, just let me know."

"Thanks, Mr. Garcia," Ruby said.

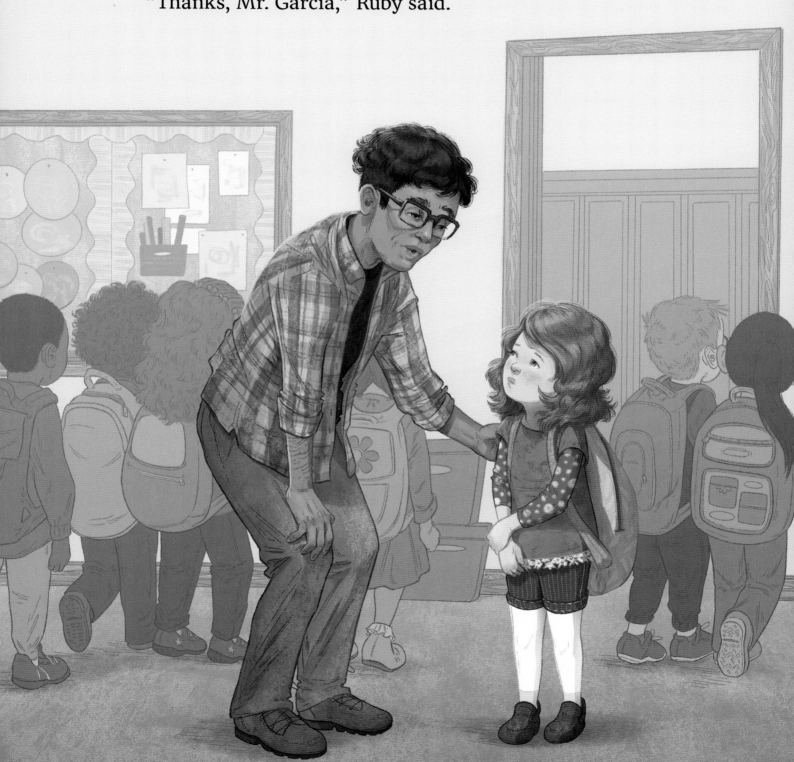

Ruby walked home, thinking about her problem.
Maybe she could at least give her problem a name,
like Mr. Garcia had said.

And so she named her problem **Lonely**.

"Hello, **Lonely**," Ruby said to herself in the mirror.

"I'm sorry that you feel so alone."

But **Lonely** didn't say anything back.

Lonely was a very quiet problem.
Kind of gloomy and sad. As if she was missing her glow somehow.

"I wish I could cheer you up," Ruby said.

The next morning, Ruby decided to bring **Lonely** to school with her.

When the other kids ran and played at lunchtime, Ruby and **Lonely** shared a sandwich and watched as the birds sang and ate their bread crumbs.

They loved watching those silly birds.

When her brother and sister were out and the house was so quiet,
Ruby and **Lonely** read their new comic book together.
It made them giggle.

When Mom and Dad were busy, Ruby and **Lonely** painted a sunset together with their watercolor set.

It turned out beautiful.

And when Lola was busy barking at birds and chasing squirrels in the yard, Ruby and **Lonely** listened to music and danced wildly in front of the mirror.

They were great dancers.

Ruby and **Lonely** started having fun every day.

One morning, a new girl came to Ruby's classroom, and Ruby and **Lonely** asked her to play with them at recess. They laughed so much!

Another day, after school, Ruby and **Lonely** brushed Lola's fur, ran with her, and gave her treats. Lola jumped all around.

The next night, they shared a special surprise for the family after dinner: homemade chocolate chip cookies and a one-of-a-kind family portrait.

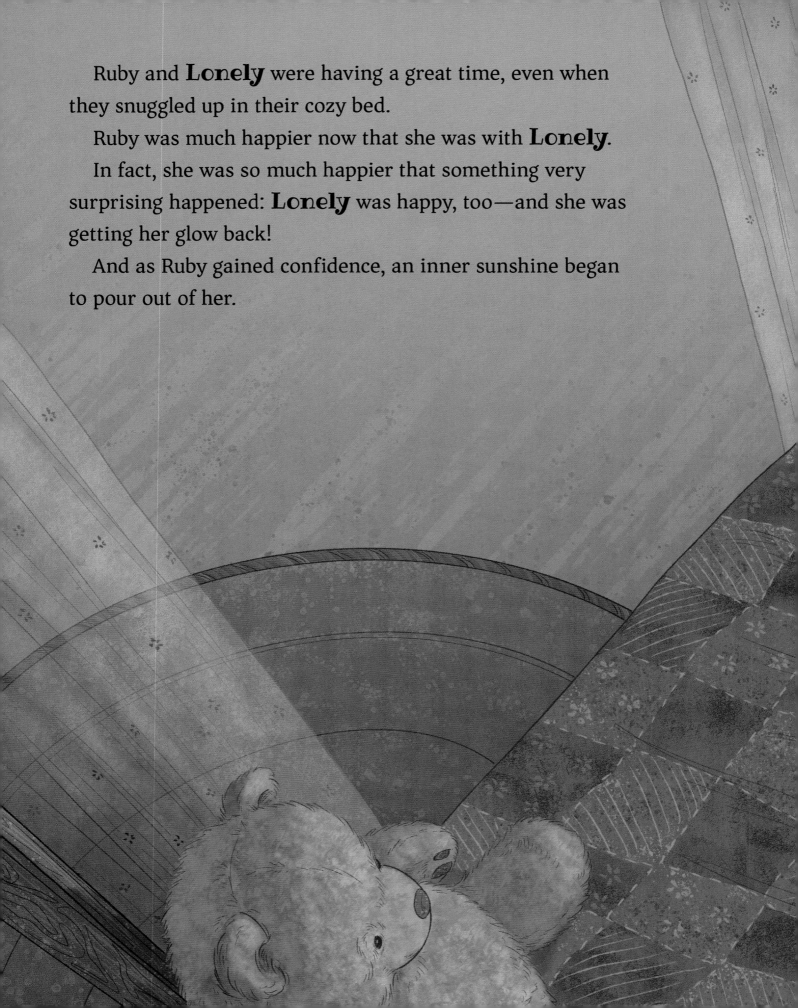

Ruby and **Lonely** were having a great time, even when they snuggled up in their cozy bed.

Ruby was much happier now that she was with **Lonely**.

In fact, she was so much happier that something very surprising happened: **Lonely** was happy, too—and she was getting her glow back!

And as Ruby gained confidence, an inner sunshine began to pour out of her.

Everyone seemed to notice. Other kids at school began to ask Ruby to play with them—and she did.

At breakfast, Ruby asked her brother and sister if they would take her out for pizza on the weekend—and they said yes!

After school, Ruby asked her mom to do crafts with her—
and they had the best time.

At night, Ruby asked her dad to start reading
with her at bedtime—and he agreed.
Ruby and **Lonely** drifted off to sleep,
dreaming of seahorses and shooting stars.

Even Lola had noticed the change in Ruby and **Lonely**.
She had started hanging out in Ruby's room more often,
happy to just lie on the bed and watch them both.
It was so nice having Lola nearby.

Ruby and **Lonely** weren't spending *all* their time
alone together anymore.

Ruby's life had gotten fuller.

As she watched Ruby branch out, **Lonely** felt warm and joyful inside. After all, she was part of Ruby, and Ruby was part of her.

And **Lonely** would always be there, waiting deep inside, whenever Ruby needed her.

Because of that, Ruby never had to feel all alone, ever again.

Ruby did not have a problem anymore. But she *did* have a new best friend . . .

forever.

A Note from the Author

Dear Beloved Readers,

Ruby and Lonely called out and implored me to write their story. As a child, I suffered intense loneliness. Raised in an unhappy home, I searched for an answer to the lonely problem. As an adult, loneliness has also been a theme. My spiritual search, my creative projects, my travels—my entire life's work— has been on a mission to heal the loneliness we all experience as humans.

Whether all alone in one's room, in a crowd of strangers, in a group of friends, or at family functions, loneliness seems to find us in many ways. Curiously (and sadly), loneliness is something we rarely talk about. I believe it's time to make it safer to talk about what we ALL feel. While we have our *Invisible Strings* that keep us connected to our loved ones forever, we still have to live with, befriend, and solve the mystery and pain of feeling lonesome.

The only relationship that we can count on 24/7 and for every single day of our lives is the one that we have with our own selves. The person looking back from your reflection in the mirror is your best friend, companion, caretaker, and creative partner in life. *You* will never leave *you*, nor are you ever really alone— because you will always have yourself. The more you get to know this beautiful inner friend and learn to love and take care of them, the freer you will be and the happier and more peaceful you will feel. I know because I can remember the exact moment I saw my own inner best friend in the mirror for the first time— and how it made my anguish fade away.

This was my great wish when I brought Ruby and Lonely together on the page—that we all could get to know the best friends who live within us and never forget them ever again.

—*Patrice Karst*

QUESTIONS FOR DISCUSSION

· Why did Ruby feel so lonely?

· How did Ruby start to feel better about being alone?

· What was it about being with Lonely that made Ruby happier?

· Why did Lonely's colors start coming back?

· Why do you think that feeling happier inside made Ruby's "inner sunshine" come out?

· Have you ever felt really lonely, like Ruby?

· What can you do when you feel lonely?

· What does it mean to be your own best friend?

· What adventures can you have with your own "inner best friend"?

· Isn't it wonderful to know that you have a best friend inside of you, too? Just like Ruby and Lonely!